Aesop's
FORGOTTEN
FABLES

For Eloïse, Ema, Felix, Julian, Linda, Natassia,
Nathan, Oriana, Sofia, Timothee and Yannick and to Malala Y. FT

For Henry Morton-Robinson with love. FMW

First published in Great Britain in 2013 by Andersen Press Ltd.,

20 Vauxhall Bridge Road, London SW1V 2SA.

Published in Australia by Random House Australia Pty.,

Level 3, 100 Pacific Highway, North Sydney, NSW 2060.

Text copyright © Fiona Waters, 2013. Illustration copyright © Fulvio Testa, 2013.

The rights of Fiona Waters and Fulvio Testa to be identified as the

author and illustrator of this work have been asserted by them

in accordance with the Copyright, Designs and Patents Act, 1988.

All rights reserved. Colour separated in Switzerland by Photolitho AG, Zürich.

Printed and bound in China by Toppan Leefung.

10   9   8   7   6   5   4   3   2   1

British Library Cataloguing in Publication Data available.

ISBN 978 1 84939 706 3

FULVIO TESTA

Aesop's
FORGOTTEN
FABLES

Retold by **FIONA WATERS**

ANDERSEN PRESS

CONTENTS

The Sheep and the Dogs

A shepherd was walking amongst his sheep one day, checking all was well with them with his trusty dogs by his side. Two of the sheep stood out a little from the rest of the flock and began speaking to the shepherd. "We find your treatment of us very odd and indeed a little unfair," the one sheep began.

"Yes, and we give you wool and milk and lambs, but all you give us in exchange is grass - and we have to look for that ourselves," added the other sheep.

The shepherd scratched his head, not quite sure what to make of this complaint. "And then we see you treating those dogs quite differently," continued the first sheep. "As far as we can see, they do nothing at all and yet you share your lunch with them."

The dogs sat up and barked at the silly sheep.

"Do nothing at all? Do nothing at all?" one said.

"What do you mean, we do nothing at all?" said the other.

"Why you ridiculous creatures, you wouldn't be here if it wasn't for us! Thieves would steal you, wolves would eat you!" said the first dog.

"In fact," said both dogs together, "if we were not here, you would be too terrified even to come out to graze!"

The sheep looked at each other foolishly and then turned quietly and walked back to join the rest of the flock.

For the dogs were quite right, and the sheep were never heard to make a complaint ever again.

BE GRATEFUL FOR WHAT YOU HAVE INSTEAD OF BEING JEALOUS OF WHAT SOMEONE ELSE POSSESSES.

The Eagle and the Crow

A crow was hopping around a field of sheep, quietly minding his own business looking for flies and insects to eat. All of a sudden, there was a great whirring of wings and a huge eagle swooped down. Reaching out, the eagle grasped hold of a lamb in his talons and bore his prize away to his hungry chicks high in their mountain eyrie.

The crow was mightily impressed with this feat. The eagle had looked so strong and graceful. The foolish crow decided that he would be able to pull off just such a trick and so he flew up into a tree and launched himself at the nearest sheep.

Unfortunately, the nearest sheep was no small lamb, but a large fat ram and there was no possible way that the crow could ever have lifted him off the ground. His claws became entangled in the ram's woolly coat and as he flapped and tried to disentangle himself, he made such a commotion that the shepherd heard and came running over to see what was going on. As soon as he saw the crow, the shepherd held on to him fast and quickly, clipped his wings and then stuffed him into a cage. In vain did the crow squawk and shriek, but he was trapped.

Later that evening, when the shepherd went home for his supper, he brought the cage with him to show his children.

"What kind of bird is that, Father?" they asked.

"It is a crow," the shepherd replied, "but he thinks he is an eagle."

And the poor crow just hung his head in shame.

IF YOU ATTEMPT WHAT IS BEYOND YOUR POWER, YOU WILL ONLY COURT MISFORTUNE AND RIDICULE.

The Crow and the Pitcher

A very thirsty crow was desperate for a drink and was delighted when she spotted a pitcher of water. She flew up to it with great joy, but then discovered that while there was indeed water in the pitcher, it was only half full, and the pitcher had a very narrow neck. But she was not about to give up so easily. She looked around and spotted some pebbles and began one by one to pick them up and drop them into the thin neck of the pitcher. On and on she went, pebble by pebble, until gradually the water reached the brim of the pitcher and she was able to drink her fill with ease.

NECESSITY IS THE MOTHER OF INVENTION.

The Fir Tree and the Bramble

High up in the mountains, a tall fir tree stood by the side of stream whose banks were covered in brambles. The fir tree was very conceited and looked down on the lowly bramble. "What use are you to anyone?" it asked contemptuously. "I am used to build many fine houses and palaces, whereas you are fit for nothing."

The bramble just ignored the boastful fir tree.

But it continued, "I am also used to make strong boats and to build secure barns for farmers to store their precious grain in. Men can't do without me."

"That may well be so, but just you wait until the woodcutters come to chop you down with their big axes," replied the bramble with some dignity. "Then what would you give to be a humble bramble rather than a lofty fir tree?"

And the fir tree had no answer to that.

BETTER A HUMBLE LIFE OF SECURITY THAN FACE THE DANGER OF CONFRONTING THE HIGH AND MIGHTY.

The Fisherman and his Music

There was once a fisherman who could play the flute very beautifully. He liked fishing well enough, it earned his keep after all, but it was music that he loved the most.

One day he had the thought that perhaps the fish might like his music too and maybe that would entice them out of the water, and straight into his nets. So he took his flute down to the shore, laid his net along the sand, then stood on a rock and began to play sweetly. He played all his favourite tunes, but not one fish appeared. He then played all the tunes his mother had taught him and a few fish lifted their heads above the water, but not a single fish hopped into his net. He was bitterly disappointed and so set his flute aside in order to cast his net into the water as usual.

To his astonishment, shoals of fish came swimming up and soon his net was so full and heavy that he could barely drag it ashore. And as soon as the fish landed, they all began to flap and dance on the sand.

"What is this?" the fisherman cried. "You were not dancing when I was playing music and now you are!"

GOOD FORTUNE HAPPENS WHEN YOU LEAST EXPECT IT TO.

The Oak and the Reeds

A huge and noble oak tree that grew on the bank of a river was uprooted by a severe storm and thrown into the water where it fell amongst some reeds. The oak was very surprised to see that the reeds were still standing after the great wind.

"I am very puzzled that you, who are so frail and slender, are still standing and have withstood the storm," it said, "while I, who am so big and strong, have been torn up by my roots and hurled into the river."

"Oh, that is easily explained," answered one of the reeds. "We reeds sway and dance in every breeze and so we know how to bend to the greatest gale. You on the other hand fought against the storm, which proved to be stronger than you."

A BIT OF GIVE AND TAKE SHOULD REPLACE PRIDE WHEN THE OCCASION DEMANDS.

Mercury and the Woodcutter

A woodcutter was felling an old tree on the bank of a river when his axe hit a knot in the trunk and flew out of his hands, landing in the water with a huge splash. The river was wide and fast flowing so he knew he had no chance of recovering his trusty axe. As he was bewailing his loss, Mercury appeared by his side and when he heard what had happened, he dived into the river and reappeared with a golden axe in his hand. He asked the woodman if it was the one he had lost. The woodman shook his head and Mercury dived once more into the river. This time the axe he brought up was a silver one. Yet again the woodcutter said it was not his either, so for a third time Mercury dived into the river and he brought up the woodcutter's very own axe. He was overjoyed and thanked Mercury profusely. Mercury was so delighted with the poor woodcutter's honesty that he presented him with the gold and silver ones as well. The woodcutter hastened home and told his wife and all his friends and neighbours of his good fortune, and there was great rejoicing in his village.

But one of his neighbours had envy deep in his soul and he resolved to gain such riches for himself, so he ran to the river and threw an old axe into the water. Mercury appeared as before and the envious man started to wail and moan that he had lost his axe and straightaway Mercury dived into the water. No sooner had he appeared with a golden axe in his hand than the envious man reached out to snatch it from him, but Mercury let it drop back into the water and then also refused to search for the original one. So the envious man had gained nothing at all through his greed.

HONESTY IS ALWAYS BETTER THAN GREED.

The Ass and the Masters

There once was a most discontented ass who felt he had a very tough time of it indeed. He worked for a gardener and had to carry heavy loads all day and if he was too slow, the gardener would beat him. And to top it all, when he was stabled for the night, he felt his food was very scanty after all his hard work. So the ass begged Jupiter to take him away from the gardener and hand him on to a new master. Jupiter sent Mercury to the gardener and told him to sell the ass to a potter, which all duly happened.

And did that make the ass happier? Not at all, for he discovered that working for the potter was even harder. The pots were very heavy, the potter was always beating him as he was too slow, and he had even less to eat at night. So once again he begged Jupiter to give him a new master. Jupiter very obligingly arranged that the ass be sold to a tanner.

But no sooner did the ass see his new master than he began to bewail his fate yet again.

"I should have been content with my former masters for they would at least have given me a decent burial when I came to the end of my days. Now I shall end up in the tanning vat!" And unfortunately he was right.

THE GRASS IS NOT ALWAYS GREENER ON THE OTHER SIDE.

The Blacksmith and his Dog

There was once a very hard working blacksmith. All day long he would toil at his forge in the great heat, wielding his huge hammers over the hot metal. He had a little dog that used to accompany him everywhere, but as soon as the blacksmith started work, the dog would curl up in his basket and sleep soundly through all the hammering and clattering of the forge. But as soon as the blacksmith stopped work, the little dog would be wide awake again and looking for food.

One day the work was especially exhausting and the forge especially hot, so when the little dog woke up looking to be fed, the blacksmith shouted at him.

"Why should I feed you, you idle dog? All the time I am working hard you are snoring away, but as soon as I stop for a bite to eat, you are wide awake and wagging your tail asking to be fed too!"

THOSE WHO ARE NOT PREPARED TO WORK DESERVE NOT TO EAT EITHER.

The Dolphins and the Sprat

The dolphins and the whales were having a terrible argument. The sea was stormy with their fighting and all the fish were hiding. All save one tiny sprat . . .

For this tiny creature thought he could stop the battle. He stepped out bravely in amongst the dolphins and the whales and tried to persuade them to separate and make friends.

But he was bowled over by a contemptuous dolphin.

"Leave us alone!" he bellowed. "We would rather all die fighting than be reconciled by a miserable sprat like you."

WHEN THE GIANTS CLASH THERE IS NO PLACE FOR THE PUNY.

The Astronomer

Once there was an astronomer who liked to go out every night with his telescope to study the sky. He was fascinated by the formations of the brightest stars and would gaze enraptured at their brilliance on the clearest of nights. During the day, he would study maps and charts and ancient books to increase his knowledge.

One night when he was walking along a path outside the town gates, he was so absorbed in the heavens that he quite failed to look where he was putting his feet. Suddenly, he tumbled into a deep but, most fortunately, dry well. He was very shaken but unhurt and began to seek a way out of his predicament; it was not long before he realised that he was trapped.

The only solution was to shout for help and hope that someone would eventually hear him. But, of course, there were not many people out and about in the night and also he was off the beaten track. The poor astronomer was growing hoarse with shouting when he suddenly heard a voice above him.

"What on earth are you doing down there?" A man's head appeared over the side of the well. Joyfully, the astronomer explained what had happened and urged the man to seek assistance in getting him up from the depths. But the man just shrugged his shoulders and replied, "If you are really telling me that you were so busy looking at the sky that you didn't bother to watch where your feet were carrying you, then it appears to me that you deserve to be at the bottom of a well." And with that, the man walked away.

LOOK WHERE YOU ARE GOING OR IT WILL BE THE WORSE FOR YOU.

The Eagle and the Arrow

An eagle was flying high up in the skies when he was spotted by a hunter hidden on the mountainside, on the look out for game. Quickly and deftly the hunter slotted an arrow into his bow, and taking careful aim, shot the magnificent bird clean through the heart. As the mortally wounded eagle tumbled to earth, he saw that the arrow was winged with feathers, eagle feathers.

"What a cruel fate that I should die thus," he cried. "And all the more so that the arrow which will be the ending of my life is fashioned with feathers from one of my own kind!"

BE CAREFULL NOT TO GIVE YOUR ENEMY THE MEANS FOR YOUR OWN DESTRUCTION.

The Boy Bathing

A man walking along the banks of a river heard a great commotion.

"Help, help! Oh, will someone please help me!" cried the voice.

The man quickened his step somewhat and looked over the wall to peer down into the water. There he saw a young boy splashing and thrashing about, clearly in distress.

"Whatever are you doing down there in the river?" demanded the man. "You must know you look very foolish."

"Thank goodness you have come," spluttered the boy. "Please, will you help me? I am out of my depth here!"

"Well, perhaps, you should have thought of that before you embarked on such a thoughtless exercise," replied the man crossly. "It is most unwise to venture out into water before knowing how deep it is."

The boy could not believe his ears.

"Please sir, I beg of you, help me out of the water first, before you start scolding me. If you do not, I am likely to drown," he pleaded.

But the man on the bank continued talking as if he were giving a lecture in the university and the poor boy was left to struggle on his own.

IN A CRISIS IT IS BEST TO GIVE HELP FIRST AND ADVICE SECOND.

The Cock and the Jewel

The cock was scratching around in the farmyard for something to eat, both for himself and for his hens, when he happened to find a precious jewel that had been dropped there. The cock was quite sure that it was a very special object, but he didn't really know what to do with it, for of what use was it to him or his hens?

"This is undoubtedly a very fine piece of great value to someone who can appreciate its worth, but I would rather have one single grain of corn than all the jewels in the world!" said the cock and walked on by.

THE VALUE OF AN OBJECT IS IN THE EYE OF THE BEHOLDER.

The Goose that Laid Golden Eggs

There was once a husband and wife who lived in the woods where they kept geese. They would take the eggs into the village to sell on market day; they never made very much money but they had enough for their needs and were contented enough.

One particular market day they needed to buy a new goose as the fox had run away with their prize goose the night before.

There were not that many for sale but one goose in particular looked at them with an especially bright eye, and they decided she was the one. The old lady who was selling her said with a strange secret smile, "Take care of this goose, she is particularly fine at laying."

The wife tucked the goose under her arm and as she walked away looked back at the old lady, but she had mysteriously disappeared as if by magic. The next morning when the wife went to collect the eggs she was astonished to find one that was pure gold.

"Husband, come quickly! The new goose has laid a golden egg!" And when the husband hurried over he found it was indeed true. And so it was the next day and the next, and the next after that.

Well, the couple now wanted for nothing. They had plenty to eat and logs for their fire at night and honey to pour over their porridge. But they were not contented; one egg a day seemed such a slow way to make their fortune, and so they decided the best thing would be to kill the goose and get all the gold eggs at once. But alas, once they cut the poor goose open they found she was just like any other inside and of the golden eggs there was not a trace.

GREED IS RARELY REWARDED.

The Bear and the Travellers

Two friends who were travelling together in a deserted part of the country were resting under a tree when all of a sudden a bear appeared up ahead. Realising that the bear had not seen them, one of the friends quickly scrambled up a tree and hid amongst the leaves with no thought for his friend and companion. When the other man saw the bear, he realised he was in great danger, but there was no time for him to hide and he knew the bear would catch him, if he attempted to run away.

So he did the next best thing. He flung himself to the ground, and held his breath, pretending to be dead, as he knew that some people believed bears would not touch a dead body. The bear bounded up and sniffed all round him, and still the man held his breath and lay perfectly still. The bear sniffed round again, and then snuffled in his ear, but still the brave man held his breath and did not move a muscle. Eventually the bear ambled off, having clearly decided that the man was indeed dead.

When he thought the path was finally clear, the cowardly man up the tree climbed down and came up to his friend.

"Whatever did the bear whisper to you?" he asked laughing loudly.

His erstwhile friend replied, "He told me never again to travel with a selfish friend who deserts me at the first sign of danger." Then he picked up his bag and set off down the road, in the opposite direction to the one the bear took, of course, all on his own.

MISFORTUNE WILL TEST THE SINCERITY OF FRIENDSHIP.

The Ass's Shadow

A man hired an ass for a journey as it was summertime and he felt his journey was too long to undertake on foot in the heat. He came to an agreement with the owner of the ass that he would come along as well to drive the animal and so the three of them all set off together. The sun beat down relentlessly and it grew hotter and hotter.

By and by the man decided that he needed a rest, so he asked the owner to stop the ass. He jumped down and made to lie on the grass in the ass's shadow, wishing to be out of the sun.

"You can't do that!" said the owner. "You have only hired the ass, not his shadow."

Well, the man wasn't having any of that. "I have hired your ass and paid you good money, so I have complete control of him during the time we are together."

As you might imagine, the owner wasn't going to accept that. It was his ass after all. Both men became crosser and crosser and their arguments became more and more heated. And it wasn't long before words became blows and there they were scrapping on the grass like a pair of dogs. The ass had been standing by patiently, but when the two men started fighting, he took to his heels and galloped off. The foolish men shouted even more, this time at the ass, but he was soon quite out of sight. So the traveller had to walk all the way to his destination, and the owner had lost his ass.

IT IS BETTER TO SHARE THAN TO END UP WITH NOTHING AT ALL.

The Peach, the Apple and the Blackberry

A peach and an apple were lying in the fruit bowl, waiting for someone to come along and choose one of them to eat. Mulling over who would be the first to be chosen, they began to discuss their relative merits; who was the juiciest and who was the most beautiful. Before long the discussion became quite heated and they were headed for a full-scale quarrel. Unseen by both of them, a humble blackberry was lying on a separate plate.

"Come, come," it said. "This is a ridiculous argument! Stop right now and let us all be friends."

THE LOUDEST QUARRELS ARE OFTEN THE MOST PETTY.

The Trees and the Axe

One day a woodman went into the forest and very politely asked the trees if they would provide him with the wood necessary to make a new handle for his axe. After due consultation amongst themselves, the largest trees, who were all oaks, considered this a modest request and allowed the woodman to take a young ash sapling to carve as the new handle for his axe. Such a small, plain and unassuming tree seemed appropriate to them for the task. But no sooner had the woodman made the new handle than he was back in the forest with his axe and began to chop down the largest oak tree of all. By the time the rest of the trees had grasped what was happening, it was too late.

As a result of the gift of the sapling, the largest tree of all lay felled on the forest floor. The horrified trees bewailed their innocence in the ways of mankind, but a fully grown ash whispered that they only had themselves to blame. Had the oaks not been so ready to sacrifice the ash, the rest of the trees might have been able to stand growing for many more years.

IN YIELDING THE RIGHTS OF OTHERS, WE MAY ENDANGER OUR OWN.

The Woman and the Fat Hen

There was an old woman who earned her keep by selling eggs from her hens. One in particular would lay copious eggs of a very fine quality indeed, and these eggs were always in demand. The old woman thought to herself, "I need to get lots more eggs from that hen and then I can make even more money." Thus she decided to feed the hen double the amount of barley every day, so that she would lay twice a day.

But as soon as the old woman put her plan into action, the hen became so fat and contented that she stopped laying altogether!

RELYING ON QUANTITY RATHER THAN QUALITY DOES NOT ALWAYS PRODUCE THE DESIRED RESULTS.

The Ass Loaded with Salt

There was a poor peddler who used to buy whatever he could find at the market and then take it home to trade with his neighbours. One day, he bought a big quantity of salt and loaded up his ass with as much as possible. On the way home, while crossing a stream, the heavily laden ass stumbled and fell into the water. When he stood up again he found to his relief that his load was much lighter, as so much of the salt had been dissolved in the water. The peddler, however, drove the ass back to market and loaded the panniers up with even more salt than before, so the ass was really weighed down.

Off they set again, back home.

But when they reached the stream once more, the wily ass immediately lay down in the water and almost all the salt dissolved. Of course, when he stood up again there was no weight at all on his back. The peddler just drove the ass back to market, but this time he bought a great number of sponges and filled the panniers absolutely to the brim. And so they set off for home again.

When they reached the stream yet again, the foolish ass wasted no time in lying down in the water. But, alas for him, this time when he stood up, the sponges had absorbed so much water he nearly drowned, and so his burden was greater than before.

And the peddler set off home with a quietly satisfied smile on his face.

YOU CAN PLAY A CLEVER TRICK ONCE TOO OFTEN.

Mercury and the Sculptor

Mercury was keen to know how well regarded he was by human beings, so he decided to visit earth to seek an answer, and by rather devious means. He disguised himself as a man and visited a sculptor's studio.

There were hundreds of statues for sale, including one of Jupiter.

"What would the price be for that statue of Jupiter?" he asked the sculptor.

"That is a crown, sir," answered the sculptor.

"Is that all?" asked Mercury, laughing at such a low price for so great a god. "And what of that one?" he said, pointing to one of Juno.

"That is half a crown, sir," replied the sculptor.

Better and better thought the arrogant Mercury.

"And what is the price of that one over there?" he asked, pointing to one of himself.

"Oh that," said the sculptor, smiling. "I will give you that one for nothing, if you will buy the other two."

BEWARE OF HAVING TOO GOOD AN OPINION OF YOUR OWN WORTH.

The Seaside Travellers

Once there were two travellers walking along the coast, high above the seashore. While they walked they gazed out to sea, far, far away towards the horizon. And as they looked, way in the distance, they saw a huge ship sailing across the ocean towards land. The travellers decided to walk towards the shore, so they could see the ship up close when it sailed in. As they continued to walk, they saw that the ship was not a huge ship at all but a small boat; they decided, however, that they would still like to watch it coming in to the harbour. But when they finally reached the harbour the huge ship was not a small boat either, it was just a log and they realised all their waiting and watching had been in vain.

OUR ANTICIPATIONS OF LIFE OFTEN OUTRUN ITS REALITIES.

The Wolf and the Horse

On his rambles round the countryside a wolf came across a field of oats.

"Well, that is no use to me at all," he said crossly to himself and continued on his way.

After a short while he met a horse.

"Just back there is a very fine field of oats," he said to the horse. "It would give me great delight to show you where it is."

"And just why would you want to do that?" said the rightly suspicious horse.

"Well, for your sake I have generously left it untouched. I would very much enjoy hearing your teeth munching on the ripe grain," said the wolf ingratiatingly.

"If wolves were able to eat oats, my devious friend, I very much doubt you would be offering me this meal," said the horse, with a disbelieving snort.

THERE IS NO VIRTUE IN GIVING TO OTHERS THAT WHICH IS USELESS TO ONESELF.

The Viper and the File

A hungry viper found himself by accident in a carpenter's shop. He searched everywhere for something to eat, but of course, there was nothing there. The poor viper then went from one tool to another, begging for something to eat. But none of them were able to help him. Then he spotted the file; he wriggled his way along the worktop, passing a pair of pliers and a chisel and an awl on his way. He flicked his tongue over the file only to hear the file snarl, "Do not try to get anything from me! It is my business to bite others and I am not changing that for a mere snake." So the snake slid off, his hunger still unappeased.

THINGS ARE NOT ALWAYS WHAT THEY SEEM.

The Vain Crow

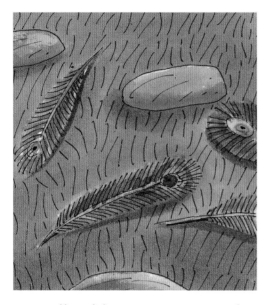

A crow was dissatisfied with his lot and sought a better standing in life. He was as vain and conceited as only a crow could be. As he hopped along the path, he came across some gorgeous and richly coloured feathers that had been dropped by a passing peacock. The crow was delighted. He picked up the feathers and carefully stuck them in amongst his own drab black ones; then he strutted up to his own flock of crows, saying gleefully, "Just look at me, you silly old crows. I am as glorious as those peacocks, and I shall be leaving you to take my rightful place with them!"

The other crows were not impressed and just shook their heads as the vain creature headed off towards the peacocks.

But as soon as he tried to ingratiate himself with the peacocks, they recognised him for the intruder he was. Very quickly, they stripped him of all the gaudy feathers. They were not gentle in so doing, and chased him off with many a peck and a buffet.

The crow recognised his utter foolishness and made his bedraggled way back to his former companions, thinking to join them once again as if nothing had happened. But they only remembered his airs and graces and were equally unwelcoming, chasing him away from the flock.

One alone stayed to give him the benefit of his wisdom. "Because you have not been content with your own feathers, you have earned the contempt of your equals and the punishment of your betters." Then he too flew off, leaving the crow alone to reflect on his folly.

IF YOU PRETEND TO BE SOMETHING THAT YOU ARE NOT, YOU WILL SURELY BE FOUND OUT AND MADE TO PAY THE CONSEQUENCES.

The Travellers and the Plane Tree

It was a scorching hot day and some weary travellers were walking along a very long and dusty road in the full heat of the sun. To their great joy they spotted a plane tree further down the road and their steps quickened as they sought the deep shade provided by its spreading branches. They flung themselves down underneath the tree and sighed in relief as the shadow of the leaves enveloped them all.

After they had rested for a while, one of the travellers looked high up to the crown of the tree and said to his companions, "When you think about it, the plane really is a useless tree! It bears no flowers or fruits and is really of no service to man whatsoever."

The plane tree was shocked by this huge ingratitude and retorted angrily, "How dare you say that, you ungrateful creature! Only a moment ago you were longing for shade and you rushed up to shelter from the burning sun under my leaves. And then while you are actually benefitting from my help, you are rude about my worth and call me good for nothing."

The traveller was shamed into complete silence, and rightly so!

A FREELY GIVEN SERVICE IS OFTEN MET WITH INGRATITUDE.

The Wolf and the Goat

A wolf was trying to find something to eat at the base of a steep rock, but there was little or nothing for him as he scrabbled among the piled up stones. All of a sudden, he heard a noise and when he lifted his head, there was a goat perched above him, grazing on the very small patch of grass that covered the tip of the rock. "Ah," the wolf thought. "Dinner!"

But he soon realised that there was no way he was going to be able to climb up the rock, it was too steep and there were no footholds at all, so he would need to entice the goat down.

"Ahem, madam," the wolf called up to the goat. "Pray do come down from this steep rock, your life is in grave danger up there. You will find there is plenty of food for you here."

But the goat was not so easily led astray.

"I very much doubt the honesty of your concern, Wolf," she said. "You could not care less whether I find good grass to eat or not. What you want is to eat me!"

KIND WORDS ARE OFTEN SPOKEN WITH AN ULTERIOR MOTIVE.

The Travellers and the Hatchet

Two men were travelling along the same road together when one of them suddenly stopped in his tracks, and picking up a hatchet that was lying carelessly in the road said, "Gracious me, just look at what I have found lying in the road. It is a hatchet!"

His companion replied rather crossly, "Surely we should share and share alike. You should say 'Look what we have found.'"

But the first man just shrugged his shoulders and tucked the hatchet under his arm.

They had not gone much farther down the road when they met up with the woodcutter, who had actually lost the hatchet in the first place.

"Hey you," he said to the man carrying the hatchet, "that is my hatchet. How dare you steal it!"

"Oh dear, what shall we do? This woodcutter looks as if he might cause us trouble," said the alleged thief.

But his companion replied, "You were not prepared to share your find with me, so it is you alone who is in trouble," and he just carried on walking down the road.

THOSE WHO DON'T SHARE THE PRIZE CANNOT EXPECT OTHERS TO SHARE THE DANGER.

The Two Pots

A great flood swept two pots away down river; one was made of earthenware and the other of brass. As they were buffeted along in the swollen river amongst all kinds of debris, the brass pot called out to the earthenware one, "Stay close by my side and I will do my very best to protect you."

But the earthenware pot replied most anxiously, "Thank you, I greatly appreciate your concern, but that is just what I am most afraid of! If I keep away from you, I will be able to float down the river to eventual safety. But if we jostle up to each other and touch only once, I will be smashed to smithereens."

EQUALS MAKE THE BEST FRIENDS.

The Thief and the Dog

A thief decided to rob a rich man's house one night. As he had done some odd jobs for the rich man, he knew the layout of his house. He also knew there was a dog in a kennel in the courtyard and he was sure the dog would start barking the moment he appeared. So the thief packed some juicy chunks of meat in his bag and, as soon as he placed his ladder against the wall of the big house, threw one piece of meat after another over the wall.

As the cunning thief expected, the dog came bounding up to where the meat had fallen, but he just sniffed it and looked hard at the thief, perched precariously on the ladder.

The dog then growled and said, "Get out of here quickly before I bite you on the leg. I have always had my suspicions about you, but this excess of generosity on your part only confirms my opinion that you are up to no good," and the faithful dog began barking loudly.

A BRIBE IN THE HAND USUALLY BETRAYS MISCHIEF IN THE HEART.

The Stubborn Goat and the Goatherd

A goatherd was trying to gather all the goats together to take them home to the fold after they had been out grazing all day. All the goats did as they were bid, and gathered together on the edge of the path, save one. She stood on top of a rocky outcrop and refused to come down despite all the goatherd's entreaties. He whistled to her, he shouted at her, he tried to lure her down with sweet clumps of grass - all to no avail.

In the end he threw a stone at her, hoping to startle her into joining the rest of the herd. But to his horror, the stone flew right out of his hand and broke one of her horns.

"Ah, please don't tell my master what happened. He will be so furious with me!" the goatherd pleaded with the goat.

She just looked down her nose at him. "You fool! Even if I don't tell him, my broken horn will," and with that she jumped down and joined the rest of the herd.

IT IS NO USE TRYING TO HIDE THAT WHICH CAN'T BE HIDDEN.

The Peacock and the Crane

A peacock and a crane happened to meet one day. The haughty peacock spread his magnificent tail feathers and looked down his aristocratic beak at the crane, who just stood motionless on his long thin legs.

The peacock said, "Just look at my truly brilliantly coloured feathers, and see how very much finer they are than yours, which are exceedingly plain and dull." He rattled his feathers down again into a splendid long tail of purple and blue and green.

The crane looked up at the peacock. "For sure your feathers are much brighter than mine, your plumage is very fine indeed. But, my dear sir, can you fly?"

The peacock pretended he hadn't heard the question and just looked even loftier.

"I thought not," said the crane. "When it comes to flying, I can soar high, high into the clouds with my plain and dull feathers, whereas you are confined to the earth just like any common farmyard cockerel!" He rose into the sky in one fluid movement, just to prove the point.

FINE FEATHERS DON'T MAKE FINE BIRDS.

The Flies and the Honey Jar

A jar of honey had been knocked over in the busy kitchen and no one had the time to mop it up. The honey slowly spread in a big pool all around the upturned jar and the sweet, heavy smell drifted around the room and out of the door into the garden. Before too long flies were buzzing around looking for the source of the heady smell. Of course, once one had found the honey the rest were there very quickly too, and the spread of honey was soon covered with flies. All of them began eating as fast as possible and gorging themselves until every last drop of honey had disappeared. But then the flies discovered that not only were they so full that they could scarcely move, but also their feet were stuck fast to the stickiness on the table. No matter how hard they tried, they could not fly away and so there they stayed, trapped until the kitchen maid came along with a cloth and hot water to clear the mess away. And that, of course, was the end of the flies too.

LOSE SELF-CONTROL AND YOU MAY LOSE YOUR LIFE TOO.

The Mischievous Dog

Once there was a dog who lived with a rich merchant who had a great many visitors to his house as he conducted his business. Instead of being grateful for being well fed and looked after, the wretched dog would snap at his master's guests and bite them with no provocation at all. In the end, the merchant fastened a great bell round the dog's neck to alert people to his presence and to stop him worrying the neighbours.

The foolish dog was very proud of the bell and took to strutting about the place, shaking his collar so that the bell would ring out. Before long, a wise old dog took him to one side and said, "My friend, the fewer airs and graces you give yourself the better. This bell was not given to you as a mark of merit; on the contrary it is a sign of disgrace."

FOOLISH PEOPLE OFTEN MISTAKE NOTORIETY FOR FAME.

The Lion and the Dolphin

A great and noble lion was once walking along the cliff tops when he caught sight of a dolphin down below, lazing in the warm water. The lion called down to the dolphin, "My fine friend, it seems to me that you have mastery of the ocean and all who live there."

The dolphin acknowledged the lion. "Indeed," he said, "as you see no one dares trouble me here."

The lion was mightily impressed. "Well, I am king of the beasts," he said. "We should form an alliance."

And so it was agreed between the two animals.

Now not long after, the lion found himself in a dreadful fight with a fierce wild bull. The fight raged back and forth and, with his strength waning, the lion suddenly remembered his pact with the dolphin and so he called out loudly for help. The dolphin sped through the water as soon as he heard the lion, but as soon as he reached the bottom of the cliff he realised, of course, that there was absolutely nothing he could do to help the lion, as he could not come up out of the sea.

In his anger the lion called down to the dolphin, "What kind of an alliance is this that we have? The very first time I call upon you for help, you fail me. You are a traitor!"

But the dolphin responded immediately, more in sorrow than anger, "Please don't blame me for not helping you. I am only powerful in the sea, I am helpless on the land, just as you would be powerless in the ocean."

YOU SHOULD ALWAYS CHOOSE ALLIES WHO ARE NOT ONLY WILLING, BUT WHO ARE ALSO ABLE TO HELP YOU.

The Leopard and the Fox

It was a warm day and a leopard was lazing in a tree when a fox came by.

"Hello, my friend," said the leopard.

The fox looked up, but didn't say a word. He did not feel the leopard was really a friend.

"Don't you think I am most handsome?" the leopard asked.

But the fox said nothing.

"Look at my fine spotted coat," boasted the leopard.

And still the fox said nothing.

"Your coat is really rather dull in comparison," said the leopard.

And then the fox spoke. "I am not especially handsome, I don't have spots and my coat may well be rather dull but my mind is very sharp indeed," and he walked on by the tree, leaving the vain leopard to contemplate his foolishness.

THE GOOD LOOKING ARE NOT ALWAYS GOOD THINKERS.

The Eagle and the Cocks

Two young cocks were fighting fiercely for supremacy over a rubbish tip. The battle raged long and hard for they were both strong and determined. Eventually, one bird gained the upper hand and soon declared himself the winner. The defeated bird slunk away to hide in a dark corner, while the victor flew to the top of a nearby barn and flapped his wings, crowing lustily all the while to declare his supremacy. But he made such a huge fuss and noise that a mighty eagle, flying high up in the sky, spotted him, swooped down and carried him away. Before too long the defeated cock re-emerged from his hiding place and took his place quietly as the king of the rubbish tip.

PRIDE GOES BEFORE A FALL.

The Moon and the Mother

Once there was a very clever dressmaker who made beautiful clothes for all her children. She would draw patterns on sheets of paper and then cut out the fabric very carefully before putting on her thimble and sewing very carefully with the neatest stitches you ever saw. She often had to work late into the night to complete a coat or a skirt for one of the children to wear the next day. One night she was bent over her cutting table, when a soft voice called her. "Mother, will you make a cloak for me to wear?"

The dressmaker looked up, very puzzled for she did not recognise the voice. Again it came, that soft voice.

"Mother, I should so like a cloak to wear."

And with that the astonished dressmaker realised it was the moon talking.

"But how could I make you a cloak that would fit you properly?" she answered, smiling up at the night sky. "Right now you are full and round, but soon you will be just a sickle sliver in the sky and in between you will be neither one nor the other," and chuckling to herself, the dressmaker took up her needle again.

NOTHING WILL EVER SUIT ONE WHO IS CONSTANTLY CHANGING.

The Domesticated Dog and the Wolf

It was a bright moonlit night and the lean and hungry wolf was out on the prowl, looking for food. He hadn't eaten for two days. As he walked along the road, he met a plump and obviously very well fed dog. Once they had exchanged the usual pleasantries, the wolf remarked, "I have to say my fine friend, life is obviously treating you very well."

"Indeed," replied the dog. "I don't have far to look for my next meal."

"So just how do you manage that?" asked the wolf as his tummy rumbled.

"Well, I just behave the way my master asks," said the dog.

"And is that very onerous?" the wolf asked.

"Not at all," grinned the dog. "I just have to guard his house and keep thieves, and any other undesirable people away. And in

return he keeps me well fed; food is always at my disposal and I have a roof over my head in all weathers."

That all sounded too good to be true to the poor hungry wolf. "Could I swap places with you for tonight?" he asked eagerly. "Life is very hard out in the forest, you know. I never know where my next meal is coming from and it is often very cold and wet."

"No sooner asked than done," said the dog. "Follow me," and he loped off down the road.

As they trotted side by side, the wolf couldn't help noticing that the dog had a mark round his neck, where the fur was worn away.

"Forgive my asking," said the wolf, "but what caused that mark round your neck?"

"That? Oh, that is nothing," responded the dog. "It is probably from the collar that is fastened to my chain during the day."

The wolf stopped dead in his tracks.

"Collar? Chain?" he demanded.

"Yes," the dog said. "I am regarded as a bit of a fierce fellow, so I am tied up during the day, but I assure you I am entirely at liberty during the night."

"So you can't move about whenever and wherever you want all the time?" spluttered the wolf.

"No, not really, but I am a real favourite, you know. Even my master feeds me off his own plate, and the children . . . "

But the wolf was gone, galloping back down the road as fast as his skinny legs could take him.

"My liberty is the most precious thing to me," he called over his shoulder. "Freedom is worth far, far more than any luxuries a master with a chain could give me."
And he disappeared back into the forest.

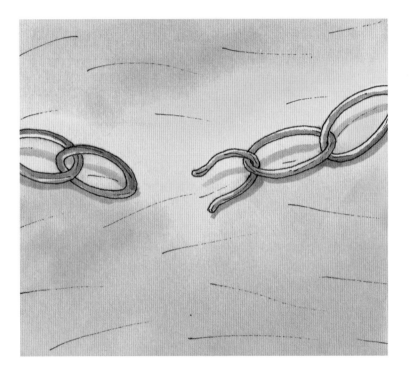

LIBERTY IN HARDSHIP IS BETTER THAN LUXURY IN SLAVERY.

FULVIO TESTA is one of Italy's most distinguished artists and illustrators, who has had many exhibitions in the United States and Europe. In addition to his own prize-winning books, he has illustrated titles by authors such as Anthony Burgess and Gianni Rodari.

FIONA WATERS was born in Edinburgh, and is famous in the children's book world for her passion and enthusiasm. She has written over eighty children's books, and won the CLPE Poetry Prize in 2007.

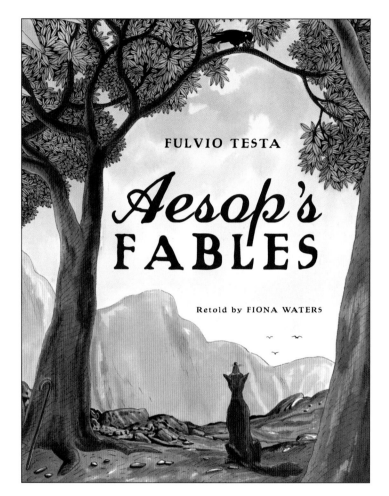

9781849390491

Also available is this stunning edition of Aesop's sixty most famous
fables, including classics such as *The Fox and the Crow,*
The Town Mouse and the Country Mouse, The Ant and the Cicada,
The Hare and the Tortoise and *The Fox and the Stork.*

'With its many comic touches, this anthology
presents once again the humour, folly, ingenuity, and wisdom
that make Aesop so durable.' *School Library Journal*